大鸟在中国

BIG BIRD IN CHINA

大鸟在中国

BIG BIRD IN CHINA

Written by JON STONE
Photographs by VICTOR DiNAPOLI

Based on the television special created by Jon Stone

Featuring Jim Henson's Sesame Street Muppets

Random House/Children's Television Workshop

Copyright © 1983 Children's Television Workshop, Inc. MUPPET Characters © 1983 Muppets Inc. All rights reserved under International and Pan-American Copyright Conventions. Published in the United States by Random House, Inc., New York, and simultaneously in Canada by Random House of Canada Limited, Toronto. *Library of Congress Cataloging in Publication Data:* Stone, Jon. Big Bird in China. SUMMARY: Big Bird and Barkley, intent on finding Fêng-Huang, the phoenix of China, learn many things about the country while they search. [1. Birds—Fiction. 2. China—Fiction. 3. Puppets—Fiction] I. DiNapoli, Victor, ill. II. Children's Television Workshop. III. Sesame Street (Television Program). IV. Title.   PZ7.S87785Bi   1983   [E]   82-62383   ISBN: 0-394-85645-7 (trade); 0-394-95645-1 (lib. bdg.)

Manufactured in the United States of America   1 2 3 4 5 6 7 8 9 0

Photograph on the top of page 14 Copyright © Morton Beebe/The Image Bank.

The pagoda pictured here is the Leaning Pagoda in Suzhou.

Big Bird was excited! Today he was going to show Barkley the picture of the beautiful Chinese bird. Since he had first seen the picture hanging in the front window of a Chinatown antique store, he had thought of nothing else. And so today, with Barkley running alongside and the usual bunch of kids tagging along, he roller-skated all the way from Sesame Street to Chinatown.

"We're almost there, gang! Wait for the WALK sign,"
shouted Big Bird.

Big Bird screeched to a stop in front of the antique store. In the window, just as he remembered, was the ancient scroll with the picture of the bird in the center.

The shopkeeper smiled when she saw that her friend had returned.

"I wanted to show Barkley the picture of the beautiful Chinese bird. Barkley, look!" Barkley attacked a flea, and Big Bird turned to the shopkeeper. "Can you tell me more about that picture?"

The woman carefully lifted the scroll from the window to read the Chinese writing on it. "Her name is Fêng-Huang, the phoenix of China, the Empress of the Southern Skies," the woman told him.

"Wow!" said Big Bird. "Does it say how a big American bird might find her?"

The woman read on: "'To find the phoenix, first you must find each of these places in China.'"

She pointed to the scenes pictured in each of the four corners of the scroll—a wall, a camel, a bridge, and a pagoda. "'At each place a monkey will give you a clue, and the four clues together will lead to the phoenix.'"

Big Bird had already made up his mind to try. "If you'd lend me that scroll, Barkley and I could find her. Then she could tell me all about China."

The shopkeeper looked down at the fragile scroll and shook her head.

"Please!" Big Bird pleaded so pitifully that the woman finally said, "Well . . . all right." She handed him the scroll. "But take good care of it."

"Wow, thanks! Come on, Barkley!" Big Bird skated out of the store. "We're going to China to find the phoenix!"

Big Bird skated back to Sesame Street as fast as he could. He took off his skates, left a note for Susan that he was going to China, and then hurried to Mr. Snuffle-upagus' cave to say good-bye to his best friend.

"I'll miss you, Snuffy," he sniffed. "But don't worry. I'll be home as soon as I find the phoenix."

Then Big Bird told all of his other friends about the beautiful Chinese bird he was going to find. Telly was worried. "But, Big Bird," he said, "there are a billion people in China. How will you ever find that bird?"

Big Bird showed his friends the scroll. "All I have to do is find the four places in the pictures here, and at each place a monkey will give me a clue. It's like a treasure hunt!"

"What will you eat?" asked Ernie.

"Birdseed, of course," answered Big Bird.

Bert thought that over and asked a logical question: "How can you eat birdseed with chopsticks?"

"I'll take a spoon," said Big Bird. Then he hugged everyone and everyone hugged him back. Barkley jumped up on Bert and left two muddy footprints on him. Big Bird waved, and he and the shaggy dog started off.

"Send us a postcard!" said Ernie.

"If you find any Chinese paper clips, bring them home for me!" yelled Bert.

"Me want rice cookie!" bellowed Cookie Monster.

"Good-bye!" they all called.

As the sun was setting over New York harbor, Big Bird and Barkley sailed under the Verrazano Bridge on their way out to the Atlantic Ocean. Their course would take them through the Panama Canal to the Pacific, and on the other side of that vast ocean lay their destination—China.

"Say, Barkley," mused Big Bird. "Doesn't this strike you as an awfully slow boat?"

"Woof," replied Barkley.

At last they reached the busy Chinese port of Tianjin. Big Bird couldn't wait for the boat to dock. "Hey, mister!" he yelled to a Chinese boatman on a little boat alongside their big one. "Would you please take us ashore?"

The man smiled in surprise at Big Bird and Barkley, and Big Bird decided that that meant yes. He and Barkley jumped off the big boat onto the little one, nearly turning it over.

But they reached the dock safely, and Big Bird thanked the bewildered boatman. Barkley bounded off the boat, and Big Bird shouted, "We made it! China!"

Big Bird thought that the best place to start his search
for the phoenix would be the capital of China, Beijing. It
was too far to walk. A car was too big, a bicycle was too
small, so Big Bird found the perfect way to get there.
Barkley loved riding in the sidecar.

When they got to Beijing, Big Bird unrolled the scroll and looked at it carefully. "Okay, Barkley. This first picture is some kind of wall. Let's find it."

Barkley followed Big Bird through the streets. They saw lots of little houses with ordinary walls. And they saw fancy walls around a gold, blue, and red archway.

They even saw circular walls on a huge building that looked like three Chinese hats stacked on top of each other. Big Bird didn't know that this was the famous Temple of Heaven. He just thought it was about the most beautiful building he'd ever seen.

Big Bird stopped in front of a red wall covered with Chinese writing. "Boy, Barkley," he said, shaking his head, "there sure are lots of walls in China."

Big Bird and Barkley strolled into a park. "Look!" said Big Bird. "People dancing!"

The people were not really dancing. They were practicing tai ji, a set of slow, graceful exercises that many Chinese do every morning before work. Big Bird tried to do tai ji with them, but after a few minutes he stopped. "I'd like to stay longer," he explained, even though he knew the Chinese couldn't understand him, "but Barkley and I have got to find a wall."

Big Bird and Barkley walked into a Chinese market, where a long line of people stood waiting to buy vegetables. Because there are very few refrigerators in China to keep food fresh, people have to shop nearly every day.

"Boy! Mr. Hooper would really like this store, wouldn't he, Barkley? Barkley? Where are you?"

Barkley was making friends with a Chinese chicken.

The two wandered on. Suddenly Big Bird shouted, "Duckies!" A group of little girls were doing the Duck Dance, which they had learned in kindergarten.

"Could I dance with you?" he asked. The little girls didn't understand English, but they smiled at him, so he joined right in. "Quack, quack! How am I doing, Barkley?" But then he remembered that he had to find the wall. "Good-bye, duckies!"

"Let's stop for a minute and think this over, Barkley.
There must be someone here who speaks American and can
tell us where this wall is." Big Bird sighed. He wondered
if he'd ever find the beautiful phoenix. And then he heard
the sound of children laughing. "Kids! I bet there's
a school near here. Maybe someone there can help us!"

They turned a corner and saw the school. The children were at recess in the schoolyard.

"Do any of you kids know where I could find a wall?" Big Bird asked. The teacher and the children smiled. "A wall!" Big Bird shouted. "You know, it keeps the ceiling from falling on the floor!" He was almost crying.

"What's the matter?" one of the little girls asked.

"No one here speaks American."

"I speak English," she told him.

"Close enough!" declared Big Bird happily. "Oh, I am so glad to meet you! What's your name?"

"Xiao Foo. It means Little Lotus. What's yours?"

"Big Bird," he answered. Then he tried to say her name just the way she did: the first name rhymed with "now" and started with a "sh" sound. Shou Foo.

He unrolled the scroll. "Xiao Foo, do you know where this wall is?"

Xiao Foo giggled. "Sure. Everyone in China knows the Great Wall. I can take you there after school."

"Oh, boy!" said Big Bird, and he told her about his search for the phoenix. Then he followed his new friend into her school. "Come on, Barkley. We're going to a Chinese school!"

Xiao Foo introduced Big Bird to her teacher.

"*Ni hao*, Da Niao," the teacher said.

"*Ni hao* means 'hello' in Chinese," whispered Xiao Foo. "And Da Niao means Big Bird."

Big Bird said his name in Chinese. He thought it was funny that it rhymed with "meow."

Xiao Foo explained that the teacher was giving a lesson in writing Chinese characters. By the end of the first grade, Chinese children must know seven hundred characters. By the time they finish elementary school, they must know three thousand.

"Wow!" Big Bird shook his head. "And I have trouble with just the twenty-six letters of the alphabet."

When school was over, Xiao Foo said, "Come on, Da Niao. I have to go home and ask my mother if I can go with you to find the phoenix."

"*Ni hao,*" Xiao Foo called as she ran into her family's courtyard.

She introduced Barkley and Big Bird to her mother and father, her grandmother and grandfather, and her cousins and aunts and uncles. In China, entire families live together in small apartments around a center courtyard. Often the grandparents take care of the children while the mother and father work.

Xiao Foo explained to her mother that Big Bird had come all the way to China to find the phoenix and she wanted to help him. All her relatives talked it over and finally gave their permission.

"*Zai jian!*" the family called.

"*Zai jian* means 'good-bye,' " Xiao Foo explained to Big Bird. She pronounced it "dsi jien," as if it rhymed with "sigh when."

Xiao Foo hugged her mother. "*Wo ai ni,*" she said softly. Big Bird didn't have to ask. Somehow he knew that *Wo ai ni* was Chinese for "I love you."

Off the three of them went, on their way to the first place pictured on the scroll, the Great Wall! Townspeople on bicycles stopped to stare at them walking down the middle of the road. Big Bird held Xiao Foo's hand while Barkley happily barked at the bicycles.

"*Ni hao!*" called Big Bird.

The people smiled and answered "*Ni hao,*" but still they stared. Finally Big Bird decided it was because he and his friends were walking. Everybody else in China seemed to travel by bicycle. Now that he had figured that out, he felt better.

Curious children stopped their play and puzzled men looked up from their work as the three travelers passed them. Xiao Foo was kept busy answering Big Bird's questions about the wall.

"The Great Wall is four thousand miles long. It was built to protect China from her enemies," said Xiao Foo.

Big Bird look around. "Everyone here is so nice. Why would China have enemies?"

Xiao Foo sighed. "It was a long time ago, Big Bird."

Big Bird's feet were starting
to hurt, and he stopped to look at
the scroll. "I don't think we'll
ever find this wall," he said to
Xiao Foo.

The little girl giggled. "Big
Bird, you're standing on it!"

"You can't stand on a wall," he
scoffed. "You'd get footprints on
the wallpaper!"

Xiao Foo laughed and pointed.
"Look, Da Niao."

Big Bird could hardly believe
his eyes.

Stretching as far as he could see was the biggest,
longest, strongest, widest wall he had ever seen.
"That's some wall!" declared the bird.

"This is the Great Wall, Da Niao," said Xiao Foo.

"Great? It's tremendous!" agreed Big Bird.

"It was all built by hand," the girl explained.

Big Bird looked puzzled. "Why didn't they use bulldozers? It would have been a lot easier."

Xiao Foo giggled. "There were no bulldozers then. The wall was started twenty-four hundred years ago and it took two thousand years to build."

Big Bird began to look around.

"Now what?" asked Xiao Foo.

"Now we have to find a monkey," answered Big Bird.

"Okay!" said Xiao Foo.

Big Bird stuck his head through an opening in the top of the wall and looked down. "No monkeys down there," he said. Then he turned around and jumped in surprise.

Standing right in front of him was somebody in a fancy suit with a face like a monkey! Big Bird kept calm and did what every brave and intelligent bird should do.

"Xiao Foo, help!" he screamed.

Xiao Foo laughed and clapped her hands. "It's the Monkey King!" she cried. "Everyone in China knows the Monkey King! We have songs and stories and books about him."

"Are you the monkey who has a clue for us?" asked Big Bird.

The Monkey King did a cartwheel and then gave them their first clue: *"The stone soldiers stand guard over the glass chessboard, while those who would find the phoenix sail silently among them."*

And he disappeared as magically as he had arrived.

Big Bird stroked his chin and tried to look wise. "I see," he said. "I see. Well, that certainly makes sense." But it didn't.

Xiao Foo didn't understand the clue either, but she did know where to find the second picture on the scroll, the camel.

"The camel is one of the statues guarding the Sacred Way to the Ming Tombs," she said. "Come on!"

"Tombs?" echoed Big Bird, his eyes growing very large. But he followed Xiao Foo anyway.

They came to a roadway lined with huge stone animals. Xiao Foo explained, "This is the Sacred Way to the Ming Tombs, and the animals are guarding the emperors who are buried there. The horse is for the emperors to ride."

Big Bird scratched his head. "For the emperors to ride? But I thought the emperors were . . . never mind."

Xiao Foo moved on to a statue of an elephant. "The elephant stands for peace," she explained.

Then she pointed to the next stone animal. "Look, Da Niao!"

"A camel!" yelled Big Bird. "Hey, wow! We've found the camel."

Then out of nowhere popped the Monkey King, and in his singsong voice he gave them the second clue: *"Past the elephant who would drink the river dry, past the see-through mountain."*

"What does *that* mean?" asked the confused bird.

But the Monkey King was gone.

Now it was time to find the third picture on the scroll, the bridge.

Big Bird was very discouraged. "'Elephant who would drink the river dry'? 'See-through mountain'? What kind of clues are those? I was expecting something like 'Look under the sofa'! Now that's a clue."

But Xiao Foo wasn't downhearted. "We still have to find a bridge, Da Niao," she said. "Let's go to Suzhou. There are lots of bridges and canals there. That's why it's called the Venice of China."

And so the travelers started out again.

When they got to Suzhou, they crossed many little bridges. The canals were crowded with boats transporting all sorts of things. Some of the boats pulled barges with heavy loads.

Xiao Foo explained that in China many people live on their boats.

They wandered through the narrow streets near the canals and saw pretty little houses and gardens. Xiao Foo said that Suzhou is such a beautiful city that the Chinese have a saying for it: "Heaven above, Suzhou on earth."

They came to another bridge, and Big Bird looked at the scroll.

"Look, Xiao Foo!" he cried. "It's the next picture!"

Before Xiao Foo could even answer, the Monkey King appeared again. He struck another pose and gave them the next clue:

"Past the feathers that
grow from the riverbank,
past the headless water
buffalo."

The Monkey King disappeared and Big Bird threw up his hands. *"Another swell clue!"* he complained. To calm him down, Xiao Foo led them into one of the lovely gardens.

Big Bird looked at some tiny trees that were growing in pots.

"Growing miniature bonsai trees is an ancient Chinese art," Xiao Foo told him.

Big Bird turned and his eyes grew wide. There, across the garden, was a beautiful pagoda.

"Look, Xiao Foo, look!" he shouted. "It's the last picture on the scroll!"

"We did it!" exclaimed Big Bird. "We found all the places on the scroll! Now all we need is the last clue."

They looked around the lovely garden for the Monkey King, but all they saw was a man telling a story to a group of children.

The three weary travelers sat down to listen while they waited for the Monkey King.

Big Bird was beginning to think that the Monkey King had forgotten all about the last clue, when the storyteller finished his tale, stood on one tiptoe, and right before Big Bird's eyes slowly turned into the Monkey King.

"Follow the clues I have given you," sang the Monkey King, "and they will lead to an ancient banyan tree. There you will find the Empress of the Southern Skies—the phoenix."

"Come on, Barkley!" called Big Bird. "We're almost to the phoenix!"

But Barkley was gone!

The great shaggy dog had run into the courtyard of an old temple. There, sitting still as statues, he found two fierce-looking animals. Barkley sniffed at them, but he couldn't tell whether they were lions or dogs. Suddenly the two lion-dogs sprang at Barkley. He was terrified! But then he realized that the lion-dogs just wanted to play.

The three romped around like old friends until Big Bird and Xiao Foo found them and told Barkley it was time to go.

They walked on, not really knowing where to go next. They had found all the pictures on the scroll, and still nothing made sense.

Suddenly Xiao Foo stopped and pointed to the water-covered rice paddies below them. "The glass chessboard!" she shouted happily.

"You're right!" Big Bird answered. "And the mountains! I'll bet they're the stone soldiers standing guard!"

"We have to follow the river through the mountains," said Xiao Foo. "That must be what the Monkey King meant when he said, 'While those who would find the phoenix sail silently among them.'"

So with Barkley and Xiao Foo in the front of the little boat, and Big Bird in the back, the three floated down the river.

They saw houses and pagodas built high on the mountainsides; they saw people pulling big boats up the river. But they didn't see the phoenix.

Big Bird laughed when he saw a funny-looking sort of mountain. "Hey, look, Xiao Foo. That rock looks like an elephant with his trunk in the water."

Xiao Foo jumped up and down, so excited that at first she couldn't speak, but then she managed to get the words out. " 'The elephant who would drink the river dry'!"

Big Bird was very proud of himself for recognizing the elephant. "Maria says that sometimes it helps to use your imagination," he announced.

They floated farther and farther down the river, looking right and left, searching for the Monkey King's clues.

Barkley barked at all the other boats and at the people on shore, at the birds and fish and mountains. He barked very loudly at one mountain and Big Bird looked up.

"Xiao Foo!" Big Bird exclaimed. "The see-through mountain!"

Xiao Foo laughed and clapped her hands. There, towering above them, was a mountain with a hole in it that you could see right through.

On they sailed, the swift current carrying them along. "Look, Da Niao! Feathers!" called Xiao Foo.

"You're right!" answered Big Bird. The bamboo trees growing from the riverbank looked just like feathers! "Only one more clue to find, Xiao Foo. Keep your eyes peeled for a headless water buffalo!"

Big Bird looked at a smooth, brown rock in the water. It moved! Then a head rose up out of the water and looked back at him. It wasn't a rock. It was a water buffalo that had been holding its breath and feeding on grass growing on the river bottom.

Xiao Foo saw it too. "When he has his head under water, you know what he looks like, Da Niao?"

"A headless water buffalo!" shouted Big Bird happily.

"We've found all the clues," Big Bird said to Xiao Foo, "but where's the banyan tree?"

A flash of color appeared on the riverbank. It was the Monkey King! "You have done well, my friends," he called. "Now come ashore to find the ancient banyan tree, and in it, as I promised, Fêng-Huang, the golden phoenix, the Empress of the Southern Skies."

Quickly the travelers steered the boat to the riverbank.

Barkley led the search for the tree. Xiao Foo tugged at Big Bird's hand. "Come on!" she said. But Big Bird was staring in awe at something he saw ahead of them.

Standing majestically in the center of a clearing was a giant tree, its branches stretching upward and outward farther than any tree Big Bird had ever seen. He knew that it must be the ancient banyan tree.

Slowly, silently, they approached the huge tree. Big Bird called softly to the phoenix, but there was no answer. Xiao Foo called to her in Chinese. Silence.

Then they heard the distant sound of many, many birds. The sound grew louder and louder, and a hundred twinkling lights appeared in the branches of the banyan tree.

The hundred tiny lights gathered into one brilliant ball and then burst. There in silent, golden beauty stood the phoenix. She stretched her wings as if she had just awakened from a long sleep. "So you have found me at last, Big Bird," she said softly. "What is it you want of me?"

Xiao Foo poked Big Bird to remind him to answer, and Big Bird spoke. "Well, at first I wanted to ask you all about China, but I found out a lot about China just looking for you."

The phoenix smiled. "I planned that, Da Niao. I saw to it that in looking for me, you met Xiao Foo here, visited her home and school, and saw the Great Wall and the Temple of Heaven. I made sure that you visited my great cities and tiny villages, met my people, and learned how to write and speak some of my language. How could I possibly have told you as much about China as you have found out for yourself?"

Then the Empress Phoenix began to sing. Her deep, rich voice filled the valley and echoed from the mountains all around. Big Bird had never heard such a sound. Every phrase seemed more beautiful than the last, and he listened, enchanted, until the song ended on a high, clear note that seemed as delicate as a crystal thread.

And as the echo of that last note died, the golden phoenix spread her glittering wings once more and disappeared in a shower of falling stars.

Big Bird bent down to Xiao Foo. "She's gone. But we found her, didn't we, Xiao Foo?"

"Yes, Da Niao," answered his new friend. "We found her. And now it's time to go home."

Suddenly Big Bird looked very worried. "Will I ever see you again?" he asked.

"I hope so, Da Niao," said Xiao Foo. "Maybe someday I can visit you in America and you can show me your country."

Big Bird smiled, but he couldn't stop a great tear from running down his beak.

Xiao Foo was almost crying, too, but she reached up and brushed away Big Bird's tear.

"*Wo ai ni*, Da Niao," she said softly.

"I love you, too, Xiao Foo," said Big Bird.

Then Xiao Foo straightened his necktie. "Come on, Big Bird, it's a long way home."